The SNOW QUEEN

By Hans Christian Andersen

Retold and Illustrated by

Richard Hess

Macmillan Publishing Company
New York

Collier Macmillan Publishers
London

To my three young muses
Lila, Jessica, Elyssa

Macmillan Publishing Company
866 Third Avenue, New York, N.Y. 10022
Collier Macmillan Canada, Inc.
Printed in the United States of America
10 9 8 7 6 5 4 3 2 1
The text of this book is set in 12 pt. Goudy Old Style.
The illustrations are oil on canvas reproduced in full color.
Library of Congress Cataloging in Publication Data
Andersen, H. C. (Hans Christian), 1805–1875.
The snow queen. Translation of Snedronningen.
Summary: After the Snow Queen abducts her friend Kai,
Gerda sets out on a perilous and magical journey to find him.
[1. Fairy tales] I. Hess, Richard, date. II. Title.
PZ8.A542.Sn 1985b [Fic] 85–42797 ISBN 0–02–743610–1

Contents

et us now begin a most amazing tale. The tale has seven parts. When we get to the end, you will know more than you do now about evil and magic, courage, kindness, and love.

He smashed
the evil mirror
and the glass
shattered into
a million bits.
All its terrible
tiny pieces
were sucked up
by the winds
and blown high
above the earth
in a great
whirling cloud.

ONE: THE EVIL MIRROR

Long, long ago, when magic and such were much more common than in our own time, there lived a most wicked demon. He was horribly, dreadfully, awfully, frightfully, fearfully, wickedly wicked. So unbearable was he that he had no name because no one wanted to be reminded of him by hearing his name mentioned. So bad was he that even other demons thought him despicable and avoided his company. He was, of course, proud of his reputation and constantly sought new ways to discomfort any and all the creatures of the earth. You can imagine, then, how very pleased he was the day he completed his most excruciating, ultimate masterpiece of mischief.

After much effort, the demon had created a looking glass. It was no ordinary mirror, for it reflected the very opposite of how things really were. Anything good and beautiful looked twisted and ugly. Things bad and evil looked attractive and desirable. In the mirror the most beautiful garden looked like boiled spinach. The prettiest of people looked repulsive: Sometimes they seemed to be standing on their heads, and other times they seemed to have no bodies at all. Faces were distorted beyond recognition. If a face had even one freckle on it, the freckle in the mirror spread everywhere, across the whole face and mouth, making that person look crooked and cruel. To the demon, of course, that was the best part of all. And he laughed and laughed and was altogether quite delighted with himself.

So pleased was he, in fact, that he began to think of ways to extend his evil joke. At last he thought of the perfect way. First he summoned up the winds from the four corners of the earth. Then, when they were howling and gusting and blowing together in all directions, he took up the mirror and, raising it high, smashed it down on the rocky ground of his lair. The glass of the mirror shattered into a million billion bits and more. All its terrible tiny pieces, each smaller than a grain of sand, were sucked up by the winds and blown high above the earth. They circled the world in a great whirling cloud. When they fell upon the land and blew into a person's eye, they stuck there

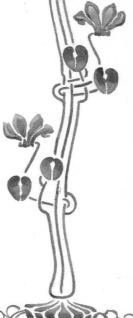

Kai and Gerda
lived in an
attic room
high up where
the rooftops
touched.
*In summer
the children
played out on
the roof under
the two rose
trees that
grew in large
window boxes.*

and distorted everything that person looked at. Bad became good and good bad. For that person, the whole world changed, because each tiny piece of the demon's glass had the same power that the original mirror had possessed. All whose eyes were touched gave up goodness and embraced evil, causing something terrible to happen inside. Little by little, their hearts grew cold, they no longer remembered how to smile, and the honest pleasures of life were lost to them.

Watching as he flew with the winds, the monstrous demon laughed and laughed until his sides ached. He thought with malicious delight of all the trouble and sorrow to come. Meanwhile, the tiny bits of the demon mirror flew around and about the world. Some do still.

TWO: THE CHILDREN AND THE SNOW QUEEN

In a crowded old village packed with so many people and houses that there was not enough room for everyone to have a real garden, there lived two poor children. They were not brother and sister, but they loved each other just as much as if they were. The boy's name was Kai and the girl's name was Gerda. They lived with their grandmother in a little attic room high up where the rooftops touched one another, with barely space for a rain gutter between them. The attic had a big dormer window that looked out over the gables and beyond, to the rolling hills and dark forests that stretched off to the north. Outside, on either side of the dormer, between their roof and the next, two large window boxes had been placed, filled with table herbs and wonderfully colored flowers. In each box a splendid rose tree grew, throwing out long tendrils that reached the window and twined around and down to the edges of the roof. In the summer, using two flat boards for benches, the children would sit out on the roof under the flowers, playing games, looking at their picture books, singing all the songs they knew by heart, and making up stories about the flowers. The roses were their favorites, and many of their stories were about them and what would become of them when summer ended.

When winter was upon the land and snow drifted between the window

The snowflake grew and took the shape of a beautiful lady all of ice, who shimmered with dazzling points of light. Her eyes shone like two clear stars, but there was no peace in them.

boxes and flowers slept under their cold white blanket waiting for the return of spring, the children sat inside, pressed against the window, looking out over the snowy rooftops. They made perfectly round peepholes by warming pennies on Grandmother's stove and then pressing them against the frosty panes. In the evenings Grandmother sat with them and told stories about how and why things were as they were. The children were filled with wonder at all she knew.

One day, when the first snow was falling fast outside, the windows slowly became covered with frozen crystal patterns that glistened in the bright morning light and changed their colors when the children moved their heads from side to side. Gazing beyond them at the swirling snow, the old grandmother pointed and smiled. "Ah," she said, "I see the white bees are swarming." The children pressed close to the window.

"Have the snowflakes a queen bee, as real bees have?" the little boy asked.

"Oh, yes," said the grandmother. "Indeed they do. She flies where the swarm is thickest. She is the largest of them all and never remains on the ground, but flies up again and again to the sky. Often, on a winter's night, she flies through the streets peeping into the windows, and the panes freeze into wonderful patterns. They are winter's flowers."

The children looked closely at the intricate, lacy designs that the frost had made, and they knew the Snow Queen had truly visited their high window.

"Can the Snow Queen come *inside* here?" asked little Gerda.

"Just let her dare!" cried Kai. "I'll put her on the stove and she will melt!"

Grandmother smiled and stroked his hair and told her stories. And so they passed a long and pleasant winter day.

That evening, after they had been tucked in for the night, Kai crept out of bed, climbed up on the window ledge, and peered out the frosty window. The snowflakes were still silently gliding down. As he watched, one of them—a very large one—landed just on the edge of the window box. To the little boy's amazement, it hovered there and then began to grow. It became larger and larger, and, as it did, took on the shape of a slender, graceful lady dressed in the finest white gauze that shimmered with tiny, dazzling points of light.

7

She was delicate and beautiful and very much alive, but she was made entirely of glittering ice. Her eyes shone like two clear stars. But they showed no contentment: If there was any peace in them, it was the peace of the grave.

As Kai watched, the ice lady nodded and made a slow beckoning gesture with her hand. When she did so, the frost sprang from the edges of the pane and the window froze over, so that Kai could no longer see clearly. The little boy was frightened and jumped down from the window. He bounded back to bed and hid beneath the covers as a shadow—as of a large bird, it seemed—passed across the window. Next to Kai in the warm bed, Gerda slept peacefully. But Kai stayed awake a long time and shivered as he thought of the strange apparition he had seen. In the morning he made no mention of the specter's eerie visit, for, as the night had passed, it had begun to seem more and more like a dream. He soon forgot all about the lady and her disturbing call.

One by one the winter days came and went, and the drifted snows gave way to the spring thaw. The warm sun shone; the swallows built their nests; green buds appeared; and people began once more to open their windows to the warm, balmy air. The children played in their little garden on the roof. In time, the roses bloomed and spread their sweet fragrance around them as Kai and Gerda sat under the blossoms in their window-box arbor and sang this little song:

> Rose, Rose, Rose, Rose,
> Will I ever see thee red
> Aye, merrily, I will,
> If spring but stay.

One afternoon—the church clock in the little town had just struck five—a dark cloud passed without warning in front of the sun. A sudden wind blew down from it, scattering the leaves and whipping the pages of the picture book the children were reading. Great gusts blew soot from the rooftops and dirt from the flowerbeds round and round them in a small whirlwind. Then, just as quickly as it had come, the wind ebbed away and disappeared. But it had left something behind.

A sudden gust blew down out of the dark cloud, whipping dirt and soot round and round the children in a small whirlwind. "Oh," cried Kai. "I have something in my eye."

"Oh!" cried Kai. "I have something in my eye." And he began to rub it.

"No, Kai," exclaimed the little girl, flinging her arms around his neck. "Let me see what it is." Kai blinked his eye and looked first up, then down, and then from side to side. But, for all her peering, Gerda could find nothing in her playmate's eye.

"I think it must be gone now," she said. But it was not. It simply couldn't be seen, for it was not a speck of sand or a bit of cinder. It was one of the tiny, silvery grains of glass from the shattered demon mirror that the winds had carried long and far—the enchanted mirror in which everything great and good looked small and nasty, and everything mean and ugly looked irresistible. Poor Kai, he could no longer feel it, but the splinter of glass was there, lodged in the corner of his eye. Everything he looked at began to be distorted by the mirror's evil power.

"Why do you look so concerned?" he shouted, jumping to his feet. "It makes you ugly! And why are you sitting under these ugly, worm-eaten roses? They're awful!" And he began to strike at the flowers and pull the petals apart and stamp on them in such a frenzy that Gerda cried out, "Kai, Kai, what are you *doing*?" When he saw how frightened she was, he laughed, shredded one last rose, and ran from the little roof garden.

From that moment on, Kai's behavior changed. He was a different boy. When Gerda got out their favorite picture book, he slapped it from her hands, saying it was only fit for babies. When Grandmother told them stories, he squirmed and interrupted with rude questions. "But," he'd argue, "but . . ."

Then he began to imitate and mock everyone who lived about them in the little town. He spoke and walked as they did—but with cruel exaggeration, making fun of their peculiarities and failings. He soon did these caricatures very well, and, of course, people laughed at him, as long as they were not his target. But when their turn came, their feelings were badly hurt by his mockery and by the laughter he provoked.

All his games were now quite different. He became sly and clever and seemed to have grown older than his years. He sought out the older boys more and more, leaving Gerda to play alone. He was inconsiderate to all, and all

With the speck of demon glass stuck in his eye, Kai became a different boy. He was rude and inconsiderate of others. He became sly and mocking and seemed to have grown older than his years.

10

because of the piece of demon glass in his eye. His distorted vision of things had begun to turn his heart cold.

One day when winter had returned, Kai took the magnifying glass Grandmother used for reading, out into the falling snow. He held out his sleeve and let the snowflakes fall upon it. "Now, Gerda, look here," he said. "Do you see how cleverly they're made?" Through the magnifying glass the snowflakes looked like geometric flowers or strangely branched stars.

"They're much more interesting and more perfect than real flowers," he said. "They haven't a flaw. Oh, if only I could save them from melting and keep them with me forever."

With that he flung the magnifying glass aside, into the drifted snow. Snatching up his little sled, he ran toward the market road where the older boys were playing. "It's getting late, Kai," Gerda shouted after him. "You shouldn't be out after dark." But Kai did not answer, so she picked the reading glass out of the snow and sadly went back inside and up the long stairs, wishing that Kai were once more the gentle playmate he had been.

Out on the edge of town, the older boys liked to slide down the slippery snowbanks to the road below. The bolder ones would hitch onto the passing farm sleds and steal a long, fast ride behind them. There was some danger involved, and they were not supposed to do it.

On this evening, right in the middle of their games, a strange, sleek sleigh, drawn by two powerful horses, turned into the road. The sleigh's runners were lacy and long. The horses' eyes gleamed red, steam puffed from their nostrils, and their polished hooves flashed and glinted as they cantered forward. A slender figure held the reins tightly, cloaked in white fur, a deep hood pulled low over the face, completely hiding the driver's features.

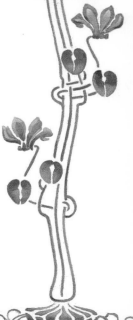

As they sped
into the night,
the driver
beckoned him
to stay.
Kai began to
be terribly
frightened.
He was stuck
fast to the
strange sleigh
that moved
with the speed
of the wind.

As the sleigh swept past him, Kai, to be daring, pushed past the other boys and threw the loop of his sled rope over a small hook that stuck out above the sleigh's back runners. As soon as the horses felt the added weight behind them, they broke into a gallop. They dashed off through the snow, pulling Kai and his little sled in their wake. As they sped into the night, the driver turned and nodded to Kai in a friendly way, as if they knew each other.

They rushed on and Kai began to be alarmed. He moved to unfasten the rope that bound him to the sleigh. But the driver again beckoned him to stay, and, feeling reassured, Kai clung tightly to his sled as the landscape hurtled past. Then, with a start, Kai realized that they had already gone miles farther from town than he had ever been before. He turned to look for the lights of the village, but they were not to be seen. The sleigh was not even on a road. It was crossing fields and empty plains circled with dark forests. Kai became very frightened. "Stop," he shouted. "Please stop!" But the horses, if anything, increased their pace. The snow falling from the sky and the snow boiling up from the runners combined into such a thick swirl that Kai could no longer see the sleigh or, indeed, his own hands in front of him clutching the runners of his sled. Somehow he managed to untie the rope that bound him to the careening sleigh. But it did not release him. He was stuck fast to the invisible sleigh as they moved with the speed of the wind. Terribly, terribly frightened, he tried to say the prayers his grandmother had taught him. But all he could remember was one verse from the little song that he and Gerda had sung together:

> Rose, Rose, Rose, Rose,
> Joy's a path to sprightly tread
> Aye, merrily, I will
> Time's swift away.

He could remember no more. And the snowflakes gathered round him, bigger and bigger, until they seemed like great white birds flapping past and wrapping their wings around him. Then, suddenly, they flew aside. The big sleigh stopped still. The driver stood up and slowly turned, hood and mantle

The big sleigh stopped still. In the moonlight Kai saw that the driver was the Snow Queen herself. "You are almost frozen," she said. "Come inside my cloak and you will not be cold."

covered with bright, sparkling crystals. Kai saw revealed before him the figure of a tall and slender woman, glittering in the brightness of the moonlight. Her eyes shone like two clear stars, and they stared straight into the little boy's wide, round face. It was the Snow Queen herself.

"We have come at a fair pace," she said, "but you are almost frozen through. Come, creep inside my cloak and you will not be cold."

Slowly he climbed aboard the great sleigh. She drew him inside the folds of her thick, furry cloak, enveloping him in its softness. He felt as if he were sinking into a snowdrift. "Are you cold now, my little one?" she asked, and kissed him on the forehead. Her kiss was as cold as ice. It reached down to his heart, which the sliver in his eye had already made cold. He felt as if he were dying—but only for a moment. Then he imagined a strange warmth flooding through him. It was the Snow Queen's spell: Although his body was just as cold as before, he simply did not feel it any longer.

Once more the Snow Queen kissed Kai, this time on the lips. And Kai forgot all about Gerda, Grandmother, his village, and all of his past life.

He gazed into her shining eyes and thought he had never seen any sight so beautiful. No longer did she seem to be made of ice, as when first he had seen her outside his attic window. As he gazed up at her now, she seemed completely perfect and not at all frightening. She smiled at him, and he felt content and secure.

Now the sleigh was moving again. "My sled," Kai murmured. "Don't forget my sled." But one of the snowflake birds was already towing it.

On raced the dashing black horses, over forests and lakes, over oceans and islands. Around them the cold wind whistled and the snow hissed. Below, the wolves howled and the black crows flew shrieking over the sparkling snow. And in the din was the echo of the demon king's laughter.

High in the sky among the stars a crescent moon shone clear and bright. Kai watched it through all the long, long winter nights. In the days he slept at the feet of the Snow Queen. Anyone seeing him sleeping there so peacefully would have thought all was well with him—except, perhaps, for the icy blue color of his skin.

On they raced over forests and lakes, over oceans and islands. Around them the cold wind whistled, and below wolves howled and the black crows flew shrieking over the sparkling snow.

High in the
sky a crescent
moon shone
clear and
bright. Kai
watched it
through all
the long, long
winter's nights.
In the days
he slept at
the feet of
the Snow
Queen.

Grandmother
and Gerda were
grief-stricken
by Kai's sudden
disappearance.
Search parties
could find no
trace of him
anywhere.
Eventually
people decided
he must be dead.
The winter was
long and dark.

Kai's disappearance was a great mystery back in the village. Grandmother and little Gerda were grief-stricken and afraid. What could have befallen him? Where could he be? The other boys told how they had seen him fasten his sled to the strange sleigh and how it had sped off into the night. Search parties were organized; other villages and towns were alerted. Word was passed around the whole countryside, but no one had seen a trace of him. He had vanished.

Gerda cried long and bitterly. Grandmother no longer smiled or sang as she went about her work. Nor did she tell her wonderful stories. Instead, she sat by the little attic window, gazing over the rooftops to the distant forests as if she expected to see him walking home. The winter was long and dark.

Eventually, people decided that he must be dead, that he must have frozen in a snowbank or fallen into a river and drowned beneath the ice. Perhaps the spring thaw would bring an answer.

THREE: THE SEARCH—THE CHERRY ORCHARD

 pring finally came, but with it no answer—though it did bring the warm sunshine. Gerda went out onto the little roof garden once more. "I don't believe Kai is dead and gone," she said to the sunshine, to the swallows, to the new rosebuds. "I don't believe it, either," beamed the sunshine. "We don't believe it," flittered the swallows. And the rosebuds wagged their heads. "No, no, we don't believe it at all," they said. That night Gerda slept very little.

Early next morning, Gerda kissed her sleeping grandmother on the cheek and left a note telling her not to worry, that she would return just as soon as she found out what had become of dear Kai. She wrapped some sugar cookies in a large napkin and set out to look for her playmate. In her pocket she carried the rose tree's first small bud.

After a long and tiring walk she came to a large river. She crawled out into the far end of a little boat that was tied up at the bank. As she looked down into the deep, dark water, she spoke to it urgently: "Is it true that you have taken my little Kai from me? Do you know where he is? Will you give

him back to me?" But the ripples only nodded and bobbed and gave no answer.

Gerda began to weep quietly and soon she cried herself to sleep. The lapping waves of the river bobbed and tugged at the boat's loosely tied rope, and the boat eased, little by little, away from its mooring. It drifted out into the main current and was soon gliding swiftly along. When Gerda awoke, she was alarmed at first to find herself lost, alone in a strange country. But then it occurred to her that perhaps this was the river's way of answering her questions. *Perhaps the river is taking me to Kai,* she thought. She ate some of the cookies she had brought and settled down to watch the banks for any sign. When night came, she slept.

She awoke the next morning, feeling hopeful, and continued to speed down the river for another day and night and then a third day. Toward sundown on the third day, the rapidly moving river began to slow. The banks on both sides were a beautiful green, dotted with bright, colorful flowers.

Around a bend, a marvelous cherry orchard appeared, surrounded by the most beautiful garden she had ever seen. In the middle of the garden was a curious house, with red and blue and yellow windows, a thatched roof, and, on either side of its split door, two great wooden soldiers presenting arms. Gerda thought at first that they were alive and called out to them. But, naturally, they did not answer. Instead, an old, old woman came to the open door and walked down to the river's edge. Her face was crinkled with age, but she had a pleasant smile. She leaned upon a long, crooked stick, and on her head she wore a huge sun hat painted with hundreds of beautiful flowers. She seemed to be wearing a bouquet on her head; it gave her a jolly countenance.

"You poor little child," said the old woman. "What brings you out into this wide world?" She walked straight out onto the water and caught hold of the boat with her crooked stick. Effortlessly, she pulled it back to the shore without even getting her feet wet.

Gerda was very glad to be back on dry land again. But she was a little frightened by this strange old woman, who obviously had magic powers. Then she smelled fresh cherry pies baking and realized that she was quite hungry. The old woman with her colorful hat was so very pleasant looking that Gerda

The woman's huge sun hat was painted with flowers. It gave her a jolly countenance. She walked straight out onto the water without getting her feet wet and pulled the boat to shore.

The table was
heaped with
cherries, pies,
puddings, and
tarts. As Gerda
ate, the old
woman began
to comb her
hair with a
wonderful
golden comb.
The magic comb
erased all
memory of Kai.

decided to trust her. She took her hand and was led into the house.

Inside, the windows were high up and made of red, blue, and yellow glass. The light coming through them bathed the room in a rich multitude of colors. The table was heaped with cherries, cherry pies, cherry puddings, and cherry tarts. The old woman smiled and told Gerda to eat her fill.

As she ate, Gerda told the old woman the story of Kai's disappearance and showed her the rosebud that she carried as a reminder of those lost happy days before Kai had changed. The old woman brought out a wonderful golden comb and began combing Gerda's long, dark hair. She spoke soothingly and said that while she had not seen the little boy so far, he was bound to come past the cherry garden sooner or later. They would simply wait for him together. "I have long wanted a little girl like you," she said. "We will be very happy together until Kai comes." She combed and stroked young Gerda's hair so that it curled and shone and rippled in the curiously colored light.

The more the old woman combed, the less Gerda could remember the reason for her search. In truth, the old woman was a witch—not a bad witch, not wicked, but she did sometimes cast spells to get her own way. Having fallen in love with Gerda, she wanted her to live forever in the garden.

Soon Gerda fell deeply asleep. The old woman placed her gently in a big feather bed that smelled of violets. As she did so, the tiny rosebud tumbled out of Gerda's pocket and fell to the floor. The old woman picked it up. Troubled, she went into her garden. Knowing the rosebud would keep Kai in Gerda's thoughts and encourage her to continue her search, the witch waved her crooked stick over all the rosebushes in the garden. They sank down into the black earth, leaving not a trace.

Gerda woke in the morning, feeling rested and happy. She played with the flowers in the garden and ate more of the delicious cherry dishes the old woman had prepared. Her long hair was combed three times a day and each night she slept peacefully, with dreams as lovely as any queen's on her wedding eve. The days passed, and, in a little while, she no longer thought of Kai at all. Sometimes it would occur to her that there was something missing from the garden, but she couldn't for the life of her think what it might be.

As Gerda saw
the painted rose,
she remembered
the lost Kai.
She began to
weep. Her tears
fell on the
empty rose bed
and the spell
was broken.
The roses burst
from the ground
in full bloom.

One day, when the old woman took off her wonderfully painted hat so that she could wash her hair, Gerda picked it up and looked at it idly, turning it in her hands. And then, suddenly, Gerda saw it! In among all the other flowers was painted a tiny perfect rose. The old woman had quite forgotten it when she had witched away all the roses in her garden. "Why, that—that's what's missing!" cried Gerda. "There are no roses here!" She went into the garden and hunted through the flower beds in vain. And as she searched, little by little she remembered Kai and her mission to find him. She began to weep. Her hot tears fell where the roses lay under the ground, and the spell was broken. All the roses reappeared again in full bloom, just as before.

"Oh, how I have been delayed," said the little girl. "I must look for Kai. I must know if he is dead or alive."

"Ah, he is not dead," said the roses, their voices riding like a distant scent upon the air. "For we have been under the ground where all the dead people stay, and he is not among them."

"Oh, thank you, thank you," cried Gerda to the roses. "Now that I know he is still alive, I must hurry to find him and bring him home again."

She picked one small bud and put it deep in her pocket. Then she ran to the end of the garden and found the gate shut but unlocked, for the old witch was not wicked and would never have tried to keep her by force. She darted through the gate and ran along the river until it turned south. There she continued to run north without quite knowing where she was going. Finally she sank down upon a big stone to rest.

She looked out across the way she had traveled. And suddenly she realized that summer was over. The trees were shedding their leaves. It was late autumn. Inside the witch's garden it had been perpetual summer. Her spells had kept the sun shining and the flowers blooming.

"Oh, dear, how much time I have wasted," Gerda whispered to herself. "Winter is coming again and I dare not rest." She sprang up and ran on.

Oh, how weary and sore her little feet became! In her haste, she had forgotten her shoes. She had left so hurriedly that she hadn't even said good-by. The air was growing colder. There were streaks and patches of snow upon

On a patch of
snow directly
before her
stood a large
black crow.
He wagged his
head from side
to side and
stared at
Gerda with an
unblinking eye.
"Caw, why are
you out alone
in the world?"

the ground. Once more she stopped to rest. There, on the snow before her, appeared the figure of a large black crow. The crow wagged his head slowly from side to side and stared straight at Gerda with an unblinking red eye.

FOUR: IN THE PRINCESS'S PALACE

The crow watched Gerda for a long time. Then he wagged his head again and said, "Caw, caw." In a deep, raspy voice he asked Gerda very politely what she was doing there and why she was out all alone in the wide world.

Gerda took a deep breath and told her story. When she had finished, the crow nodded his shiny head thoughtfully and said slowly, "It might be he. Oh, yes, indeed, it just might be."

"What? Do you think you might have seen him?" cried the little girl, and she began hugging and kissing the crow until he feared that she would squeeze the life from him.

"Gently, gently," he squawked. "Yes, it might be your little Kai who has gone to live in the palace with our beautiful Princess. But he may have forgotten all about you and his past life, for he lives in royal splendor there."

The crow told her how a young boy had come hungry to the palace gate and so charmed the young Princess with his cleverness and sweet nature that she had given him a place next to her in the palace. Now, he said, they were inseparable playmates.

"What did the boy look like?" asked Gerda.

"Well," said the crow, thinking, "he had a jaunty walk and his eyes shone just as yours do. He had straw-colored hair that curled upon his neck and was always in need of a combing. His clothes were poor, and he carried a bundle on his back."

"It must have been his sled! Oh, that's he! That was Kai!" cried Gerda with delight. "I've found him, I've found him!" And she clapped her hands and danced with joy. Then, out of breath, she turned back to the patient crow. "Will you take me to the palace?" she asked. "Please, please, so that I may see him again."

"Well," said the crow, "that's easier said than done, for a barefoot little girl like you would never be admitted."

"But if Kai knows I'm here," said Gerda, "he'll come out and fetch me. I know he will."

"All right, all right," the crow answered. "There might be a way. For I have a sweetheart who lives at the palace, a tame pet to the Princess. I shall go and ask her advice on how best your mission may be accomplished." He gave Gerda instructions about the path to follow to the palace. With that, he flew off. It was late in the evening before he returned to her.

"Caw, caw," he cried in greeting. "My sweetheart sends you her blessings, and I have brought a small loaf for you from the palace kitchen."

Gerda took it from him gladly. As she ate, he told her his plan.

"Now," he said, "it will be impossible for you to gain direct entry to the palace: The guards in silver and the palace lackeys in gold would never allow you to pass. But don't worry, my child. My sweetheart knows a back staircase that leads to the sleeping rooms, and she knows where the key is kept."

They hurried along until they came to the brightly lit palace. They slipped quietly past the guards at the main entrance and crept into the garden. Late at night, as the palace lights went out one by one, the crow led Gerda to a back door that was standing ajar.

Poor Gerda's heart beat with anxiety and longing. She felt just as if she were about to do something wrong. But she knew she had to take this chance of seeing Kai. How else could she be assured that he was happy?

"Oh, it must be Kai!" she murmured under her breath. She remembered his smiling eyes, his curling hair, and his clever wit as they sat beneath the rose trees at home. He would be so pleased to see her and to hear what a long way she had come to find him.

At last they stood upon the curving stairs. A little lamp was burning, and, in the glow it cast, Gerda could see the tame crow standing on the uppermost landing. She was twisting and turning her head for a better look at Gerda and her guide. Gerda curtsied to her, the way her grandmother had taught her. Politely she bid the lady crow good evening.

At last they stood upon the curving stairs. A little lamp was burning and, in the glow it cast, Gerda could see the tame lady crow standing on the uppermost landing.

"How charming you are. My betrothed has spoken very well of you, my dear young lady," the Princess's pet crow said gravely. "Now, if you'll take the lamp, I will lead the way."

She stepped out in front of them. Silently they passed through many beautiful chambers hung with rich tapestries. At length they arrived in a large room that was obviously the Princess's sleeping room. Like a great golden palm tree with crystal leaves, the ceiling spread above. Two beds hung from it, each like a lily hanging from a golden stem. One was white, and in it slept the dainty Princess. The other was red, and it contained—to Gerda's mounting excitement—the figure of a sleeping boy. Gerda bent slowly over the bed and held the lamp close. There was the same little brown neck she knew so well!

She could not contain herself. "Oh, Kai, oh, Kai," she cried aloud. The boy woke and turned his head. As the light fell full upon his face, she saw at once that he was not Kai at all!

"Oh," said the boy, sitting bolt upright in his bed. "Who are you? What's happened?"

By now the Princess was awake, too, and out of her bed. Her face flushed with sleep, she angrily demanded an immediate explanation for the presence of a rude and poorly dressed girl in her sleeping room at dead of night. "And what are *you* doing here?" she exclaimed, pointing an accusing finger at the two crows.

At this, poor little Gerda burst into tears. Sobbing, she told them the story of her disappointments and all that the kind crows had done to help.

"You poor child," said the Princess when she had heard her story. Her heart had been touched by Gerda's courage and simplicity. She was no longer angry with the two crows who had given her help. Indeed, she thanked them for what they had done, though she warned them never to make so light of her privacy again. As a reward for their kindness she pronounced that they were to have permanent appointment to her court, with full kitchen rights.

Gerda was finally, gently put to bed in another room. She folded her hands, warm beneath the blankets, and, drifting off to sleep, thought drowsily, *How fortunate I've been and how kind everyone is to me.*

The next morning she awakened to the sound of flapping wings. The two crows were perched upon the footboard of her bed, softly cawing to one another. "Get up, get up, you slugabed," said the wild crow when he saw that she was awake. "You have slept long, and there has been much business this morning. Thanks to you, and with the Princess's permission, my sweetheart and I were married while you still lay dreaming."

Gerda leaped from her bed and congratulated them both. Then she washed and with the two crows went downstairs, where the Princess was waiting. Gerda, the Princess, and the boy ate breakfast together at one end of an enormous table in a room lined with royal portraits. The Princess, when they had finished their meal, invited her to stay at the palace for as long as she wanted. "The three of us can play together," she said, "and you can have whatever your heart desires."

"Oh, no, thank you," said Gerda. "I can't. I must continue my search for Kai, Your Highness. I am very grateful," she went on, "for all the things you've offered me. But all I need for my journey is a pair of boots and a warm coat, if . . . if . . ."

The Princess laughed. "Of course you may have them," she said. And she fetched for Gerda, not only a coat and boots, but also a fur muff to keep her hands warm.

When Gerda was dressed, the Princess led her to the great doors of the palace. There, standing in front of the door, was a gold-trimmed coach with a coachman, two footmen, and an outrider—all in gold epaulets—waiting beside it. They were the Princess's gift to Gerda, to help in her search for Kai.

The Princess and her tow-haired playmate helped Gerda into the coach and wished her good fortune. The tame crow spread her wings and bowed deeply. "My husband will go with you a little way," she said. "But I must say good-by now, my dear young lady. I confess I have a small headache from all the excitement."

The wild crow hopped up the steps into the coach, and he and Gerda waved to their friends as the coachman whipped up the horses. The two of

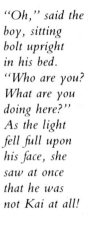

"Oh," said the boy, sitting bolt upright in his bed. "Who are you? What are you doing here?" As the light fell full upon his face, she saw at once that he was not Kai at all!

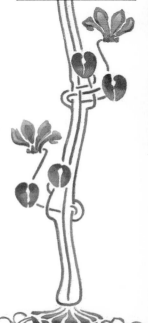

As the coach approached their hiding place, the robbers rushed from ambush and surrounded it completely. They seized the horses by their traces and dragged them to a quick halt.

them talked together fondly as the miles passed. Then he, too, said, "It's time for me to say good-by." The coach stopped, and tears welled in their eyes as they sought for words of thanks and remembrance. Then the crow flew out through the coach's open window and took up a perch at the top of a tree beside the road. He went on flapping his great black wings until the carriage, glittering like gold in the sunshine, passed from sight.

FIVE: THE ROBBERS' CAVE

When they had gone a great distance, they came at last to a dark forest in which there lived a band of robbers. The robbers had seen the coach's golden trimmings from afar, flashing and sparkling in the brightness of the sun. As the coach approached their hiding place, the robbers rushed from ambush and surrounded it. They seized the horses by their traces and dragged them to a halt. They killed the coachman and the footmen and put the outrider to flight. He fled back down the road, his terrified horse lathered and shiny with sweat.

In the lull after the slaughter, the old robber queen dragged Gerda from the carriage and drew a long, sharp knife from the scabbard at her side. "Ah, she is young and tender," she said, running her knife's edge lovingly across the palm of her own hand. "I think that I will eat her." The old hag was a horrible sight to see. She had a long, scraggly beard and great, bushy eyebrows that hung down over her eyes. Gerda was sure that this day was her last.

But the old hag suddenly let out a piercing scream. A small figure had appeared as if from nowhere, hurtling at her, leaping upon her back, and biting at her ear. It was the robber queen's young daughter.

"You shall not eat her," cried the girl. "I want her, I want her. And you shall give her to me. She can play with me and sleep in my bed. And she will give me her fur muff for my very own." Her mother, yowling with pain, tried her best to shake off the little scamp. But the girl twisted and bit and held on to the hag's ear with her teeth. Finally the robber queen was forced to agree. "All right," she growled as the gang of thieves gathered about her, laughing.

The little girl scampered down from her perch and confronted Gerda. "You are mine!" she said.

The girl was no taller than Gerda, but she was much broader and stronger, with straight black hair and piercing black eyes. She threw her arms around Gerda and said, "No one here, *not one*, shall harm you as long as you behave yourself, my little princess. But if you don't behave, I shall eat you myself." With this, she shoved Gerda into the carriage, and they were driven deeper and deeper into the darkness of the forest.

With the robber girl plumped down beside her, Gerda did her best to explain that she wasn't really a princess at all, in spite of the grand coach in which she had been riding. She told the long tale of her adventures and the disappointments she had faced in her search for Kai. The robber girl listened attentively and nodded her head. Then she dried Gerda's eyes, stuck her own hands into the soft warmth of the muff, and said nothing.

At last they arrived at a vast, dark cave where the robbers lived. A big fire was burning in the middle of the stone floor, with the smoke drifting up to an unseen hole in the ceiling. Soup was boiling in a big cauldron and rabbits were roasting on spits. The robber girl took Gerda to the farthest corner of the cave, which was spread with straw and the girl's sleeping rugs. "Tonight you shall sleep with me and my little pets," she said.

At first Gerda could not tell what pets she meant. Then she heard a nervous fluttering all around her. When her eyes adjusted to the darkness, she saw a hundred wood pigeons that had been disturbed when the girls entered and now were settling back to sleep. Nearby, watching them with wide, frightened eyes, was a reindeer. There was a thick leather halter tied around its neck. The robber girl teased the reindeer by touching and tickling it with the sharp point of her long knife. It made her laugh to see the creature's fear.

After a while, the two girls crawled into bed, and the robber girl stuck her knife into the pillow between them. She questioned Gerda about her search and why on earth she had been to all that trouble. She had never known anyone to perform an unselfish act, and it seemed somehow to disturb her.

Soon the robber girl rolled over and went to sleep. Gerda, however, could

She heard
a nervous
fluttering all
around her.
When her eyes
adjusted to
the darkness,
she saw wood
pigeons above
and, nearby, a
reindeer with
frightened eyes
watching
her anxiously.

not sleep. The robbers were gathered around the fire, arguing and laughing, trying on bits of the uniforms they had taken from the coachmen. Meanwhile, the hideous old queen was turning somersaults. It was a frightful sight.

Then, through the darkness, there came to Gerda's ear the sound of soft voices. "Coo, coo," whispered the wood pigeons, "we have seen little Kai, we have seen little Kai. He rides in the Snow Queen's sleigh all over the land. She drove over our forest when our little ones were in the nest. She breathed on them, and they all died. Coo, coo. Kai rides with the Snow Queen."

"What are you saying? Why is he with her? And where was she going, do you know? Oh, tell me, tell me, please!" cried Gerda.

"To Lapland she was going," trilled the wood pigeons, "where the land is always covered with snow and ice. Ask the reindeer. He has been there."

"Ice and snow," breathed the reindeer. "Lapland is a splendid place for snow and ice. You can run and jump and frolic to your heart's content in its great sparkling valleys. The Snow Queen has a summer castle there, although her main castle is near the North Pole, on the island of Spitzbergen. Lapland or Spitzbergen—she is bound to be one place or the other."

"Oh, my poor little Kai," sighed Gerda.

But then a shrill voice interrupted. "Lie still and be quiet or I shall stick you with my knife," said the robber girl.

Gerda pulled the covers up around her neck and, still thinking of Kai and the Snow Queen, sank into sleep.

In the morning, a shaft of sunlight from the cave's entrance awakened them. The robber girl jumped up and began to question the reindeer. "Do you know where Lapland is?" she asked.

"Who should know better than I," said the reindeer, his eyes dancing, "for in Lapland I was born and bred, deep in the snowfields."

"Listen, then," said the robber girl. "The men have left; they have gone to dispose of the carriage. Only my mother is here. Soon, though, she will be taking a nap. And then I will do something for you."

She crept across to where her mother was lying and greeted her by pulling on her beard. "Good morning, my own dear nanny goat," she said as she poured

She led the reindeer to the entrance of the cave. Then, with a stroke of her long sharp knife, she cut the thick leather halter and cried, "Run now, run with the wind!"

her mother a drink from last night's wine skin. Her mother drank greedily from the cup handed her and gradually became very drowsy. She nodded forward into her pillow and soon was fast asleep.

The little robber girl returned. "Reindeer," she said, "I have decided to set you free—but on condition that you take this girl with you to Lapland, so that she may look there for her lost playmate. I'm quite sure you know all about it, anyway, for you are always eavesdropping."

The reindeer jumped into the air and kicked up his heels with joy. The robber girl then lifted Gerda up onto his back. She gave her a cushion for a saddle, slipped on her fur boots, and handed her the old hag's fur mittens. "I shall keep your fur muff," she said, "because it is so cozy. And I shall have something to remember you by."

Gerda wept for joy.

"Oh, don't make such faces," said the robber girl. "You're supposed to look happy. Here," she said, "you'd better take this loaf of bread and these sausages if you don't want to starve."

When everything was loaded up and tied to the reindeer's back, the robber girl led the reindeer quietly across the floor of the cave and gently opened the gate at its entrance. She softly whistled for all the robber band's big dogs. She tickled the reindeer one last time with her long, sharp knife. Then, with a stroke, she cut the thick leather halter and cried, "Run now, run with the wind. And mind you take care of my little girl."

Gerda stretched out her hands—big mittens and all—toward the robber girl and shouted, "Good-by."

The reindeer leaped off, through the great forest, over rivers and valleys, as fast as he could go. Around them, the wolves howled and the ravens screamed as they sped on through a sky full of strange fire. "My Northern Lights," said the reindeer, peering back over his shoulder at Gerda. "My own dear Northern Lights. See how they flash and shine. They are the lights the Snow Queen burns at the top of the world to brighten the winter night."

Day and night, he rushed on and on. The loaf was eaten and the sausages, too. By the time they arrived in Lapland they were tired and hungry.

The reindeer
leaped off
as fast as
he could go.
They sped on
through a sky
full of strange
fire. "My own
dear Northern
Lights," said
the reindeer.
"See how they
flash and
shine!"

"They are the lights the Snow Queen burns at the top of the world to brighten the winter night." He rushed on and on. By the time they got to Lapland they were tired and hungry.

SIX: THE LAPP WOMAN AND THE FINN WOMAN

ust beyond the border they stopped at a poor and simple hut to rest and ask directions. They were greeted by an old Lapp Woman who was drying strips of codfish over a whale-oil lamp. Gerda was so overcome by cold and exhaustion that she could hardly speak. The reindeer told her story for her, starting, of course, with his own, which he considered far more important.

"You poor creatures," said the kindly Lapp Woman, when he had finished. "You've got a long way yet to go. You must now travel hundreds of miles to the top of the world to the Snow Queen's northern palace. For that is where she is now, burning her Bengal lights for us to see to the south."

When they had eaten and warmed themselves by her fire, the old Lapp Woman took up one of the codfish she had been drying. She wrote some strange markings upon it. Then she gave it to Gerda, saying, "Take this, child, and, if you find her, give it to my sister, the Finn Woman. She will help you to reach the Snow Queen's castle."

Next morning they thanked the old woman, and she wished them a fond good-by. Then the gallant reindeer sprang away again toward the tracery of beautiful lights flickering in the northern sky.

Over lakes and valleys they sped once more. Then the reindeer stopped and pointed with his right antler to a curious spot in a deep valley below. All they could see was a thin thread of smoke curling out of the deep mantle of snow. When they came nearer, they saw a chimney poking up from a large snowdrift. Gerda knocked on the chimney. Right up through the smoke appeared a large, round face smiling gaily in welcome. Gerda knew immediately that they had come to the right place. The face was smudged with soot and surrounded by matted hair, but it looked uncannily like that of the old Lapp Woman. "Excuse me," Gerda said. "But are you the Finn Woman?"

"Oh, yes," said the woman, pulling herself up to the lip of the chimney.

Gerda gravely handed her the message from her sister, written on the strip of dried codfish. The woman read it quickly, and then said, "Come in," before

Gerda knocked on the chimney, and right up through the smoke a large round face appeared. It was soot-smudged but smiling in welcome. "Excuse me," Gerda said. "But are you the Finn Woman?"

She lifted the lid of the pot, and the dried codfish seemed to whisper in her ear. "The sliver of demon glass must be removed from Kai's eye to defeat the Snow Queen!"

disappearing back through the smoke. Again it struck Gerda that she was the same woman with whom they had spent the night in Lapland.

Gerda and the reindeer made their way down the chimney as best they could and found themselves in a large and cozy room with a very high ceiling. The room was very warm. Indeed, it was so hot below the ice and snow that the Finn Woman wore hardly any clothes at all. Gerda at once took off her coat and mittens to cool down. Since the reindeer had no clothes to shed, the Finn Woman gave him a piece of ice to put on his head. Then three times she reread the message that was written on the codfish, until she knew it by heart. When she was done, she popped the fish into the supper pot that was steaming on the stove, since she made it a habit never to waste anything.

Gerda sat wearily by the warm fire and soon fell asleep. So once more the reindeer told their stories, beginning again with his own. The Finn Woman blinked her eyes, but she said nothing.

Finally the reindeer said into the silence, "You are so wise and clever. I have heard it told that you can bind the four winds of the world with a single strand of your sewing thread. Won't you give the little girl a potion so that she will be able to overcome the wiles of the Snow Queen and rescue Kai?"

"The strength of a hundred men would not help her," said the Finn Woman slowly, putting another piece of ice on the reindeer's head. Then she stood up and leaned over the stove. She lifted the lid on her cook pot, and the dried codfish swimming within it seemed to whisper in her ear. "Little Kai," she said, turning, "is with the Snow Queen, and he is delighted with everything that he finds there. He thinks that he is in the best place in the world, for he has a splinter of demon glass in his eye and his heart has turned as cold as ice. If the sliver be not taken from his eye, he will never become truly human again, and the Snow Queen will keep her power over him."

"But can't you help little Gerda with something that will give her the power to bring the Snow Queen to defeat?"

"I can give her no greater power than she already has," the Finn Woman said. "Don't you see how great it is? Don't you see how men and beasts are prompted to help her when she wanders into the wild world with her feet bare?

43

The reindeer
gently set Gerda
down and
sped back the
way they had
come. Gerda
stood alone,
without shoes
or gloves, in
the freezing
cold at the
top of the
world.

She is powerful already because her heart is pure, because she is an innocent child. She alone can conquer the Snow Queen and remove the splinter from little Kai's eye. We have no power that can help her."

With this, she gently awakened Gerda and fed her some of the special codfish from the pot. Then she led Gerda and the reindeer back up the chimney to the deep snow outside.

"The Snow Queen's gardens," she said, "begin just two leagues to the north. There," she said, turning to the reindeer, "you will find a large bush with red berries growing upon it. You must leave Gerda there and return here as fast as you can. Go quickly now, for the Queen is presently away. Gerda must find Kai and revive him before she returns."

The Finn Woman turned back toward Gerda and smiled. Without saying another word, she kissed the girl's cheek and lifted her up onto the reindeer's back. As they sped furiously northward, Gerda could see her standing by the smoking chimney waving to them.

Gerda clung to the reindeer's back. "But wait," she cried. "I've forgotten my boots." And, "Oh," she said, "I haven't got my mittens. We must go back."

But the reindeer dared not stop after the Finn Woman's urgent words. He ran until he came to the bush with red berries. There he gently set Gerda down. He kissed her on the mouth, and great tears trickled down his cheeks and froze on his whiskers. Then he turned and sped back the way they had come.

Gerda was all alone. There she stood, without shoes or gloves, in the middle of the freezing cold at the top of the world.

SEVEN: THE SNOW QUEEN'S PALACE

lowly she began to run. She ran toward the lights in the northern sky. She ran through what the Finn Woman had called the Snow Queen's gardens, which were great spreading trees with snow-laden branches bent and frozen into fantastic shapes and forms. She ran over one hill and then another. Then, from the top of the last hill, she saw in the eerie light a gigantic, brooding, icy castle. It

45

Suddenly, from across the plain, a whole regiment of snowflakes converged upon her. They were monstrously shaped of dazzling snow crystals. They were the Snow Queen's guard.

was as big as a mountain and topped with craggy turrets and towers with walls of ageless ice and drifted snow. The windows and doors were piercing winds.

Gerda's heart nearly stopped at the sight of the Snow Queen's stronghold. But she knew that somewhere within was her beloved Kai. She summoned her remaining strength and courage and plunged on. Suddenly, from across the plain, a whole regiment of snowflakes converged upon her. They did not fall from the sky, for the sky remained clear and bright. No, they swept along the ground, and the nearer they came, the bigger they appeared to grow. Gerda was reminded of the snowflakes under Grandmother's magnifying glass. But these snowflakes were not pretty and still. They were monstrously shaped and alive! Some looked like gigantic boars with great tusks; others, like seething bundles of knotted snakes; still others, like hideous, towering bears. And all of them were white and dazzling, made of snow crystals. They were the Snow Queen's guard, determined to prevent Gerda from approaching the fortress.

Poor little Gerda! She was filled with terror as the snow monsters buffeted her and lapped about her. Her breath came short and swift, in quick little gasps that began to freeze into clouds of icy mist. Urgently, she began to say her prayers, and as she did so, trembling with fear, she saw the clouds of her breath gathering and growing and taking on the shape of a band of winged warriors with swords and shields. Emblazoned on every shield were the same strange marks the Lapp Woman had written on the codfish—the very codfish that the Finn Woman had later given her to eat.

The warriors moved before her to attack the fearful snowflake monsters. Like a wave of flame, they pierced straight through them, cleaving their ranks and shattering their strength. The snowflake monsters fell away before the onslaught and were scattered once more into the thousands of snowflakes they had been before their demonic transformation. Those that touched Gerda's flushed cheeks melted into tears that splashed onto her frozen hands and feet, magically warming them. With this, her guardian army faded back to mist. Once more Gerda was alone in the clear night before the great dark castle.

Meanwhile, inside the endless halls of the Snow Queen's bleak palace, a small figure sat alone. It was Kai. The palace had more than a thousand rooms

*The icy castle
was gigantic
and bleak.
The walls were
made of ageless
ice and drifted
snow. The
windows and
doors were
piercing winds.
There were
more than a
thousand rooms
and corridors.*

A small figure
sat alone in
the bleak ice
palace. It was
Kai, turned blue
with the cold.
The Snow
Queen had
kissed away
his feelings
and his heart
was little
better than a
block of ice.

and an equal number of corridors, the longest stretching several miles. Each room, each corridor, was lit by the Northern Lights, and each was immense and cold and glitteringly empty. In the middle of this icy maze of rooms and corridors there was a great frozen lake that had cracked and buckled into a thousand thousand pieces of ice—each exactly like all the others. And here it was, at the cold heart of the never-ending empty halls, that the Snow Queen sat when she was at home.

Here, now, sat Kai. He was blue with cold, but he did not know it, for the Snow Queen had kissed away his feelings and his heart was little better than a block of ice.

As Gerda struggled toward him, he was sluggishly moving about, dragging together into a clump the sharp, flat pieces of ice, trying to fit them together into a pattern. Every one of these ice pieces transfixed him. He thought them the most beautiful things he had ever seen. He was lost to true beauty because of the splinter from the demon mirror in his eye.

Laboriously he moved the pieces into new arrangements, first one and then another, for the Snow Queen had told him that if he could discover the pattern that spelled *eternity*, he would become his own master and have all the world for his own. Try how he might, he could not discover it. No pattern he found satisfied him.

He was alone, alone in a world of ice. The Snow Queen had flown off to sprinkle snow on volcanos far to the south. And she had left him in the dreary isolation of her magic castle, to work his puzzle by the vast frozen lake. He sat and pondered, moved an endless succession of pieces, and then sat and stared again. You might have thought him frozen solid there, alone in the icy void.

That was how Gerda found him as she stepped out of the maze into the great frozen hall at last. She looked across the icy waste, and, for all his distance, for all his eerie stillness and the blueness of his skin, she knew him at once. She ran across the field of ice toward him and flung her arms about him, crying, "Kai, oh, Kai, oh, dearest Kai, I have found you at last!"

But Kai responded not at all. He sat there still, rigid, cold, and unspeaking.

Great tears spilled from Gerda's eyes, down her cheeks, and onto Kai's

She flung her arms about him, crying, "Oh, dearest Kai, I have found you at last!" But he sat rigid and cold. Tears spilled from Gerda's eyes onto Kai's breast, thawing his frozen heart.

neck and breast as she held him, sobbing. And little by little the warmth of her tears falling on his chest reached Kai's heart, thawing and melting the coldness within him. He shifted and stirred. From where she had hidden it, Gerda took out the rosebud she had brought with her from the garden. She held it steadily before his eyes. "Kai," she said, "do you remember? Oh, please remember." And she sang the little verse that had meant so much to them:

> Rose, Rose, Rose, Rose,
> Will I ever see thee red
> Aye, merrily, I will,
> If spring but stay.

The sound of her sweet voice and the words she sang touched Kai's newly warmed heart. His eyes slowly came alive as he remembered. And he, too, burst into tears. So thick and fast did the tears come, coursing down his cheeks, that in their passage they dislodged and swept away the little piece of demon glass that had so long distorted his vision. For the first time now, he saw Gerda clearly and knew her. He shouted for joy. "Gerda, Gerda, my beloved Gerda! Where have you been so long? And where have I been? What's happened to us?"

Slowly he looked around. "How cold it is here!" he said. "How empty and horrid!" But then he hugged Gerda and they laughed and wept and danced for joy. They whirled about over the pieces of ice that littered the lake. They kicked the pieces and spun them and bounced about on them. And soon the pieces of ice were moving with them, leaping with a rhythm of their own, flying through the air, shaking and trembling with the children's joy.

When Gerda and Kai were finally exhausted, they flopped down, laughing, upon the ground beside the lake. And when they did so, the pieces of ice settled down upon the surface of the lake, forming the perfect shape that Kai, by himself, had never been able to find, the pattern that spelled *eternity*. The pieces of ice had come to rest in the shape of an enormous heart. For only true love is eternal. And only the truly human heart can know true love.

Kai's tears swept the demon glass from his eye. The children laughed and danced for joy. They kicked and spun the pieces of ice and sent them flying through the air.

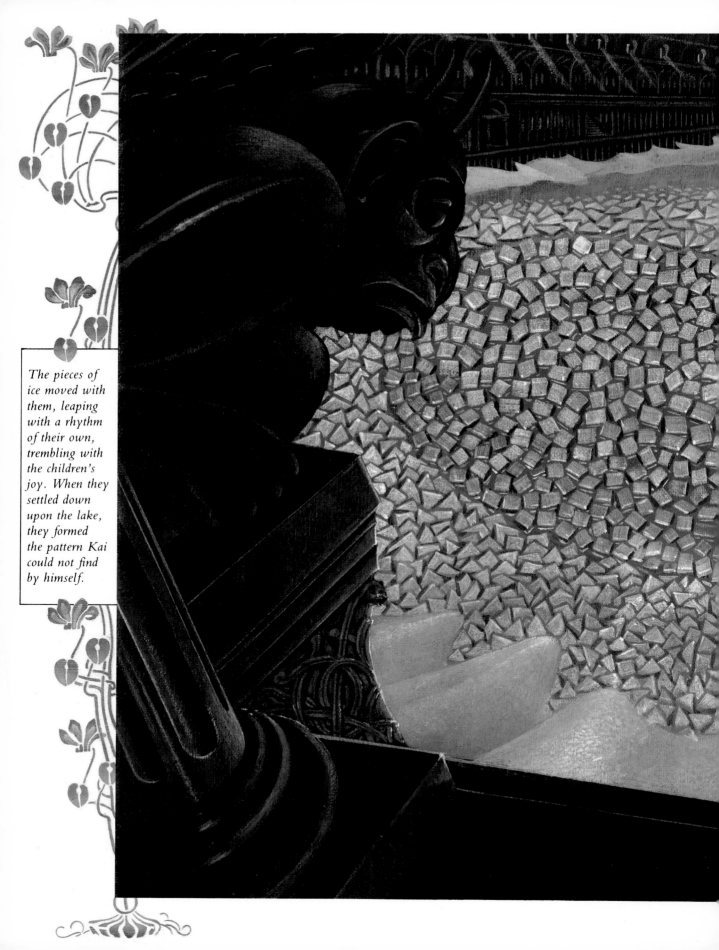

The pieces of ice moved with them, leaping with a rhythm of their own, trembling with the children's joy. When they settled down upon the lake, they formed the pattern Kai could not find by himself.

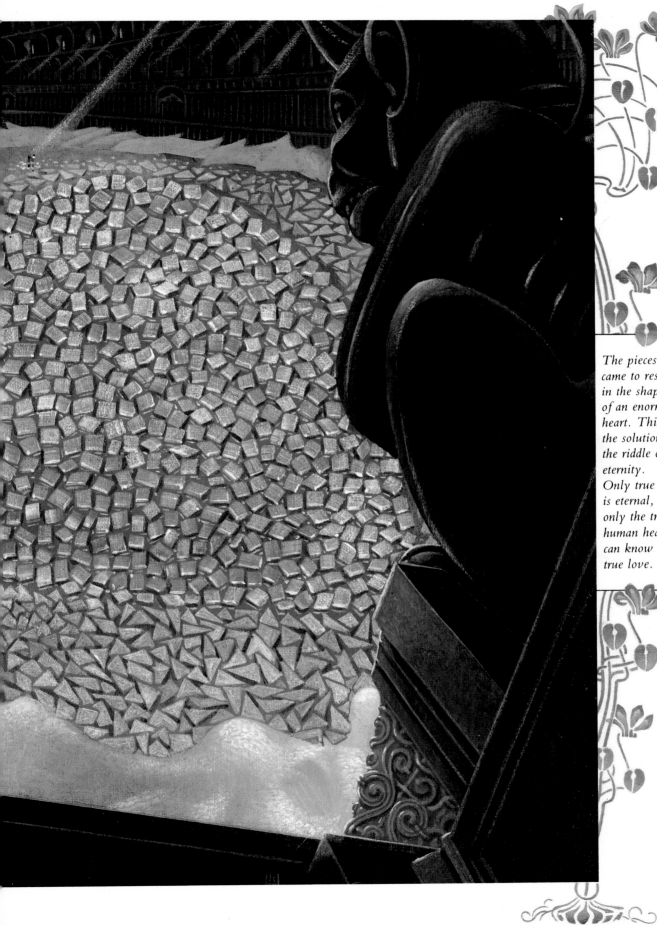

The pieces
came to rest
in the shape
of an enormous
heart. This was
the solution to
the riddle of
eternity.
Only true love
is eternal, and
only the truly
human heart
can know
true love.

Behind them the castle seemed to shudder and heave. In the doorway was the frightful specter of the Snow Queen. Angry mists swirled about her, and the eye of the demon flashed with rage.

As Kai lay there beside the frozen lake, Gerda kissed his cheeks and they grew rosy. She kissed his eyes until they sparkled like hers. And then, warmed and glowing, they walked hand in hand through the icy rooms and corridors of the Snow Queen's palace until they came once more into the light.

Outside, the winds were still and a bright sun appeared on the horizon. As they walked toward the sunrise, the castle behind them seemed to shudder and groan and heave. They turned to look, and there in the doorway they saw the frightful specter of the Snow Queen. Angry mists swirled about her. At her back was a gigantic, shapeless mass whose piggish red eyes flashed and glowed with rage and frustration. It was the demon king.

Fear stricken, the children turned to run. But the two furies seemed rooted to the spot, unable to pursue them. Then Gerda and Kai realized that the demon king and the Snow Queen could do them no further harm. The sign of Kai's release, the symbol of love, stood out on the surface of the frozen lake. Thus it would stand forever while the sliver of glass from the evil mirror would remain frozen in the eternal ice at the top of the world.

Gerda and Kai struck out across the snowfields confidently. Together they reached the bush covered with red berries. There the reindeer was waiting for them with Kai's little sled. The reindeer carried them both to the house of the Finn Woman, where they scrambled down the chimney and found food and rest and celebration. The next day, with the reindeer drawing the sled, they made their way to the Lapp Woman's hut. And again, as they laughed and ate together, Gerda was struck by the mysterious similarities between the two sisters, down to the same specks of soot in their hair. A day later, with the Lapp Woman and the reindeer for company, they moved on. They journeyed to the boundaries of the Lapp Woman's country, where they spoke their tearful good-bys, promising to visit each other whenever they could.

Then Kai and Gerda started south, where the fields were beginning to grow green with spring. As they traveled, they came to a forest bursting into bud. From among the trees, suddenly a horse leaped forth. Gerda instantly recognized it as one that had pulled her lost gold-trimmed coach. Upon its back, with a pistol and her long knife in her belt, sat the little robber girl.

Kai and Gerda
headed home
to Grandmother.
They renewed
the friendships
made along the
way. They bade
fond farewells
to the crow and
the princess, the
Finn Woman,
the cherry witch,
the robber girl
and reindeer.

She vaulted down to the ground, embraced Gerda, and then sat down with them while Kai and Gerda told their stories. She had one of her own, for after Gerda had escaped from the robbers' cave, the Princess's guard had arrived in force, led by the outrider who had managed to get away. They had taken prisoner every one of the robber band except the robber girl. They had let her go in thanks for the help she had given Gerda.

The three children traveled together until they reached the cherry orchards guarded by the two wooden sentries and the old woman who watched over them. They greeted her gaily and joyfully ate all the cherry dishes she had waiting there for them. The little robber girl bloomed with happiness at all the small kindnesses that the good witch showed them. When the time came to leave, the robber girl announced that she would stay with the old woman, to keep her company for a while.

After a long and pleasant journey, Gerda and Kai finally came to the little village that they had left so long before. On the road to the town gate, they were recognized. People rushed out to meet them. The bells in the town's tall towers began to ring out a welcome. Slowly they walked through the well-remembered streets, surrounded by a laughing, happy crowd.

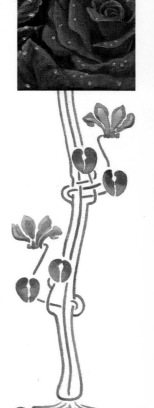

Soon they stood before the doors of their own humble home. They joined hands as they climbed the stairs and opened the familiar door. And there was Grandmother, waiting for them, weeping tears of joy. They embraced and laughed and all talked at once, and laughed some more. The children told Grandmother all that had transpired and described the wonders they had seen. They were overjoyed to be reunited, and everything became once more as it had begun. The cold, empty grandeur of the Snow Queen's palace passed from their memories as all bad dreams do. The three sat and held hands in the little roof garden, surrounded by the roses that were in bloom once again.

> *Rose, Rose, Rose, Rose,*
> *Will I ever see thee red*
> *Aye, merrily, I will,*
> *If spring but stay.*

F
AND   Andersen, Hans Christian
       THE SNOW QUEEN

DATE DUE

OC 17 '88			
SE 25 '89			
OC 23 '90			
MY 7 '91			